The Party Frock

JENNY OLDFIELD

Illustrated by Dawn Apperley

Hodder
Children's
Books

A division of Hachette Children's Books

Hodder Children's Books
A division of Hachette Children's Books
338 Euston Rd, London NW1 3BH
An Hachette UK company
www.hachette.co.uk

1

"OK, so I don't get the princess dress," Pearl argued.

"And no handsome prince," Lily pointed out.

"Just a big, bad wolf," Amber reminded her.

Pearl tutted and twirled in her red cloak. "You two are such spoilsports. I've already told you I had a brilliant time on my first

5

visit to Red Riding-Hood world!"

"That was a week ago." Amber stood in front of the dressing-up box in her basement. "I thought you'd had enough time to get sensible."

"But I still want to go back," Pearl insisted. "It's cool – there's a river and a sweet little village."

"And a wolf," Lily muttered.

Pearl ignored her. "There's a castle on the hill, and it's sunny and there are flowers everywhere."

"And a *wolf*!" Amber stood guard over the box.

"Listen. Wolfie doesn't scare me any more." Pearl took off the red cloak. "Please let me open the lid, Amber. I want to find a magical skirt – something that will whoosh me back there!"

"No way, Pearl!" Lily went to stand next to Amber. "It's too dangerous!"

"Girls, girls!" Amber's mum came down the stairs with orange juice and cookies. "I can hear arguing. What's going on?"

"Nothing, Mum. We're OK," Amber said, quickly going to fetch the tray.

"You didn't sound OK. I heard Lily saying something was dangerous. What are you three planning?"

Pearl and Lily shook their heads. "Nothing!" they chorused.

Amber's mum frowned. "Are you sure you're not up to something?"

"Sure!" Amber, Lily and Pearl insisted, their hearts in their mouths. If a grown-up found out about the magical dressing-up box, they were sure that their dream journeys would be over.

"Well, try to play nicely. Choose some dressing-up clothes, invent a nice game like you usually do." Sighing, Amber's mum went back upstairs.

"You heard what your mum said!" Pearl told Amber. "Choose some dressing-up clothes." She lifted the heavy lid and rummaged.

Lily bit into a chocolate-chip cookie. "We're only trying to help you, Pearl," she mumbled through the crumbs.

Pearl chucked out a couple of glittery belts and a squashed velvet hat. "No good . . . no . . . nope!" Then she picked out an old-fashioned shopping basket and a pair of red clogs and put them to one side, next to the red cloak. "I'll keep those."

"We don't want Wolfie to get you," Amber tucked into a custard cream.

"Don't worry, he won't. What about this?" Pearl held up a green and red striped skirt then tried it on. She slid her feet into the clogs, put on her cloak and picked up the basket.

"Here, Pearl, have a cookie." Lily offered her the plate.

Without looking, Pearl picked a gingerbread pig. *Crunch!* She bit off a leg.

A bright light whooshed out of the box and surrounded Pearl. The light began to glitter.

"Oh no!" Amber cried, running to grab Pearl's hand.

"Oh yes!" Pearl began to feel dizzy and

she dropped the ginger pig. "It's happening! Yippee!"

The light grew brighter still. It filled the basement.

"Come back, Pearl!" Lily yelled.

But Pearl felt as if she was floating and drifting on a silvery cloud. Her head was in a spin and her red cloak was caught in a strong breeze, carrying her high into the air, away from Lily and Amber.

Grandmamma, here I come! I'll save you!
Pearl thought as she was whooshed away.

Bump! She landed with a jolt on the
village green. Her empty basket rolled
across the grass.

"Hello, Red Riding-Hood. Head in the
clouds as usual and tripping over things!"
Hans called from up the top of a ladder.

Pearl picked herself up and brushed

herself down. She saw that all the cottage doors were open and the villagers were hanging up brightly-coloured flags, fixing a maypole, and setting out long tables at the edge of the green. "What's happening?" she asked.

"Tut, where have you been since dawn?" Hans asked, coming down the ladder. "Didn't you hear the Duke's herald blow his silver trumpet and announce that

there was to be a party?"

Pearl shook her head. "What kind of party?"

"A christening," Hans explained. "The Duke and Duchess want us all to celebrate their baby's naming ceremony. They're going to call him Max."

"When?" Pearl gasped. She remembered the purple Duchess and her miserable baby only too well.

It had been Pearl's job to go up to the castle on the hill and make the baby smile. But a loud noise had startled him and made him cry. The Duchess had swooped into the nursery and had Pearl thrown out into the forest where the hungry wolf prowled. That's what kind of woman she was – heartless and proud.

"Tomorrow," Hans explained patiently. "That's why I'm up a ladder, stringing lines of flags between the trees."

Just then, a group of tubby men carrying trumpets and tubas marched towards the green. They were wearing hats with narrow brims and leather shorts with braces that strained over their fat bellies.

"Here comes the brass band," Hans said. "I expect they need to practise."

Oompah-oompah! The men began to play loudly, puffing out their red cheeks and making their instruments bellow.

"Ouch!" Pearl covered her ears.

14

"More chairs needed!" Anna the milkmaid cried, dashing off to Farmer Meade's house.

Oompah-oompah!

"Who will make the pies and the cakes for the Duchess's party?" Miller Brown called from his cart. "I've brought two sacks of flour from the mill."

"Leave them here with me, Miller Brown." Red Riding-Hood's mother came to her door. Spotting Pearl, she called to her. "Red Riding-Hood, I need you to go to your grandmother's house and bring back jam for the tarts, bottled fruit for the pies and dried raisins for the cakes."

Oompah-pah! Oompah-pah!

Same old, same old! Pearl thought with a sigh as she imagined the trek through the dark wood. *Except for the party – I suppose that could be exciting.*

Her mother waved her across. "Quick as you can, slowcoach!"

"I'm on my way!" Pearl called.

Music and maypole dancing – yes, it sounds cool, Pearl thought as she set off briskly across the meadow towards the wood.

And, "Food, food, food!" she trilled as she climbed the stile. Yummy pies, tarts and cakes. Jellies, cream and custard!

"Good morning, Red Riding-Hood!" the brown cows in the meadow called. "You seem to be in a good *moo-ood*!"

"You bet I am!" she replied. "The Duke and Duchess are having a party!"

"Will there be *moo-oosic*?" A cow with a

bell around her neck came up to Pearl.
"Will there be dancing?"

"Both," Pearl promised. "Tomorrow.
Everyone is invited." She waved goodbye to
the cows and entered the wood. "Now,
what did Mum ask me to fetch from
Grandma's? Jam for tarts, fruit for pies . . ."

"Hello, Red Riding-Hood!" Two red
squirrels scuttled down a tree trunk and sat
on the path, their bushy tails twitching.
"Watch this!" They scrambled up a tree
trunk and scampered along a branch, right
to the tip. The thin branch bent and
swayed. The squirrels leaped through the
air and landed in the neighbouring tree.
"Wasn't that fun?" they cried.

"Cool!" Pearl smiled, walking on and
leaving the chattering squirrels to their

games. "Good morning, hedgehog!" she said to the next animal who crossed her path.

"What's *good* about morning?" the grumpy hedgehog grunted. "I like the

night best, when the moon is bright and I grub along the ground looking for worms and beetles!"

Pearl paused to watch Mr Grump

waddle off into the long grass. "Get some sleep," she called after him. "You'll feel better after you've had a rest."

On through to the edge of the wood she went, where she spied the tall wooden mill and her grandmother's tiny cottage beyond. "Grandmamma!" she called loudly. "It's me – Red Riding-Hood! Yoo-hoo – are you there?"

"Jams, jellies, cakes, scones!" Pearl's grandmother made a list of treats for the party. "Tell your mother I'll roast hams and make game pie, bake bread and churn fresh butter. Then, later this afternoon, I'll start on the fruit flans."

"Stop, Grandmamma!" Pearl scooped Tilly the cat from under her grandmother's feet. "Even you can't get all that done in one day!"

"Says who?" The old woman rolled up her sleeves and put on her apron. She got out her mixing-bowls, her flour, eggs, milk and sugar. "Stoke up the fire, Red Riding-Hood, so the oven gets nice and hot!"

Soon Pearl couldn't see through the clouds of flour.

"This is how you make scones," Gran said. "Pour the flour and raisins into this bowl, add the butter and eggs, stir the mixture well."

Pearl followed her grandma's instructions. "How will you carry all this food to the party?" she asked.

"Miller Brown will bring it on his cart, and I'll ride beside him and arrive in style." Brushing the flour off her hands, Grandmamma closed the oven door. "I shall wear my red bodice and my best blue skirt with *three* starched petticoats . . ." Suddenly the old woman stopped and cast an eye over Pearl's shabby striped skirt. "My dear, you need a new dress for this party!"

"Oh!" Glancing down, Pearl realised that her grandmother was right. "But I think it's too late . . ."

"Too late – fiddlesticks!" came the reply. "I'll make a dress for you in no time – a dress with frills and flounces and ribbons and lace!"

No sooner said, than Pearl's grandmother took out a tape and measured Pearl from top to toe.

"What will you make it out of?" Pearl asked, dizzy from being spun round.

Gran rushed to a wooden box under the window seat and pulled out lengths of red satin and yellow silk, white muslin and cream lace. "Leave it to me, Red Riding-Hood!" she cried. "I will make you a gown fit for a princess!"

3

The next day Pearl woke before dawn.

She'd dreamed she was Cinderella going to the ball in a sparkling dress and shiny glass slippers. Everyone had gasped when they saw her dance with Prince Charming and said, "How pretty! How very lovely she is!"

But then she woke up in her tiny bedroom, snuggled under the patchwork quilt, and she remembered where she was. "I'm Little Red Riding-Hood, and it's party day!" she exclaimed, throwing back the covers and fumbling in the dark for her striped skirt and red clogs.

As soon as she was dressed, she crept downstairs.

"Ah, you're up early!" her mother greeted her.

The kitchen fire was crackling brightly. Baby Tommy lay awake in his crib.

"I promised Grandmamma I'd go and collect my new party dress," Pearl said.

Red Riding-Hood's mother folded clean baby linen and piled it neatly on the table. "Don't leave until the sun is up. I don't want you to walk through the wood in the dark."

Pearl was itching to see her new dress, but she stayed in the cottage until the sun rose. "Can I go now?" she asked, reaching for her red cloak and escaping from the house.

"Watch out, what's the hurry?" Hans demanded as he unloaded logs from a handcart.

Pearl had almost crashed into her next door neighbour. "Oops, sorry!"

"Ouch!" Hans dropped a log on his foot. "That's OK, don't worry, I'll just hobble along . . ."

"No, really, I'm sorry." Pearl blushed as she picked up the heavy log.

"As I said, I'll hop to the party . . ." Hans limped beside Pearl as she pulled up her hood and set off for the meadow. "Ouch –

ooch – ouch!" Then suddenly he ran ahead.

"There's nothing wrong with your foot!" Pearl brushed past him. "Listen, I'm serious – I have to dash."

"To your grandmamma's?" Hans asked, laughing.

She nodded. *To collect my new party dress!* she thought. But she didn't tell Hans, who wouldn't understand about dresses and all the princess stuff.

"Well, watch out for Mister Wolf in the wood!" he called after her. "Look out for his yellow eyes and his big teeth, and don't stop to talk to anyone on the way!"

As if! Pearl remembered Hans's warning as she crossed the meadow and climbed the stile. "I know how to take care of

26

myself," she said out loud.

"Hello, Red Riding-Hood!" The squirrels and rabbits greeted her in the dawn light and invited her to chat, but today she didn't stop. She ran lightly between the trees, thinking of a dress that sparkled in the sun – a princess dress like the ones Amber and Lily had worn.

"Red Riding-Hood, stop a moment!" a gentle voice called.

Pearl turned. "Who's there?"

"Come with me!" the voice called from a thicket of willows.

"Where are you? I can't see you!"

"Please help. Come this way!"

Pearl frowned and stopped to think. Could this be a trick? Would Wolfie be able to put on a sweet voice to try to lure her off the path?

"You don't know me, but I know you." A spotted deer stepped from the willow bushes, her big eyes wide with fear. She trembled as she drew closer.

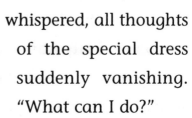

"Don't be scared," Pearl whispered, all thoughts of the special dress suddenly vanishing. "What can I do?"

"Come. I will show you," the deer replied, turning and retracing her steps into the thicket. "The hedgehog told me you were passing. He said you would be able to help."

"I'll do my best." Pearl pushed her way

through the bushes. Under her feet the ground grew soft and damp.

"It happened yesterday at dawn," the deer explained. "The Duke and his men came hunting with their bows and arrows."

"I didn't hear them." Pearl crouched low, under a thick branch, deeper still into the wood. She realised it must have happened before she got whooshed here.

"Hush!" the deer warned. She pricked her ears and listened. "We must make sure that no one is following."

When she was satisfied that they were alone, the deer went on. Eventually she led Pearl to a dark corner of the wood, in the shelter of an overhanging rock. Then she stepped aside.

Cautiously Pearl went forward into the shadows. She sensed that she wasn't alone – that another creature breathed and watched silently.

At last the creature spoke. "Red Riding-Hood, look this way – amongst the ferns."

Following the sound of the deep voice, Pearl made out the shape of the stag whom she had met in the woods once before. She saw his huge antlers and noble head, and to her horror, an arrow embedded deep in his side.

"Oh!" she gasped. "You're wounded!"

The stag lowered his head. "The arrow is deep," he told Pearl. "The Duke and his huntsmen took good aim and hit me, but I swam the river and put the hounds off the scent. I found shelter here in the wood."

"And here he has stayed for twenty-four hours," the doe explained. "But as long as the arrow remains in his side, he will not recover. You, Red Riding-Hood, must grasp it between your nimble fingers and pull it out."

At first Pearl shook her head. "I'm scared to do that!" she whispered. "What if I make it worse?"

"If you do not help, he will die," the doe urged before she withdrew from the shadows to keep a lookout. "You are his only hope."

Left alone with the stag, Pearl drew close. Though he was injured, his voice was steady and his spirit strong.

"You have helped me once before," he said. "And now it is time to prove that you are a true friend."

"I am, I swear!" Pearl replied.

"You are young," he said. "Have you learned to be brave in your short life?"

"I think so," Pearl whispered, gazing into the stag's eyes.

"Then dig deep and find your courage now," the stag told her. "For you will need it to do as I ask, and it must be done soon, because I feel myself grow faint. Before long I will be beyond help."

Pearl frowned as she felt down the stag's neck and across his shoulder until her fingertips touched the arrow.

The stag's gaze didn't waver. He seemed to see beyond the dark shelter. "Let me tell you what I am thinking of. I see the sun rising over the mountain top and the sky turn pink. I hear water running in a clear stream . . ."

Slowly but firmly Pearl's hand grasped the shaft of the arrow. *I need all my strength*, she thought. *I must pull hard.*

"The deer run through the forest at dawn," the stag went on. "They are swift and beautiful . . ."

Pull! Pearl told herself. *Pray that the arrow doesn't break!*

The stag did not blink. "I see the sun rise high over the trees . . ."

"Yes," Pearl murmured as she tugged the arrow free – cleanly, all in one piece.

The stag shuddered. "Bravely done!" he sighed.

"Will you stay here and stand guard?"

Pearl asked the faithful doe who kept watch in the willows.

Pearl had fetched water for the wounded stag to drink then pressed broad leaves over his wound and bound them in place with fronds of fern – the best bandage she could make out of what lay close by. Then she had stripped twigs from the bushes and built him a kind of den.

"I will rest while the wound heals," the stag had told her.

"And this den will hide you from the hunters if they come back to find you, and from the Wolf, if he happens by," Pearl had explained.

"I will stand guard," the doe promised. "If there is danger, I will run to find you, Red Riding-Hood."

"Good." Pearl took a deep breath. "Especially if Wolfie is snooping around – come and tell me straight away."

"Go now, my dear," the stag said from inside his den. He sounded weary. "All will be well if we know you are close by."

So Pearl said goodbye and went back to the path, looking over her shoulder many times, and keeping a wary eye out for the Wolf.

4

Pearl hurried on to her grandmother's house. She hoped and prayed that the stag's den would keep him safe from harm.

"Yo-oo can do-oo no more," the wise owl said as he left the wood with Pearl and flew ahead to the miller's barn, where he would sleep all day. "Now think ahead to the party and enjoy yourself with the rest of the villagers."

Nodding, Pearl went up her grandmamma's garden path. "Yoo-hoo!" she called. "It's me – Red Riding-Hood!"

"Ah, there you are, my dear," her grandmother said, hurrying in through the back door with a basket of fresh eggs. The kitchen table was piled high with cakes and biscuits, the oven gave off the smell of still more baking.

"Good morning, Grandmamma!" Pearl breathed in the yummy scents. She looked around hopefully for her new party dress.

"Take the fruit cakes out to Miller Brown's wagon," her grandmother instructed. "Cover them carefully with paper so the rascally mice don't nibble them."

Pearl did as she was told, saying good

morning to the cheerful miller, then running back into Gran's kitchen. "Er-hum!" she coughed.

"Is that done? Now carry out the gingerbread biscuits, and don't drop any."

Once more, Pearl carried the tray outside.

"Good. But oh dear, time is speeding by. At this rate, it will be noon and I won't be dressed for the party!"

"Talking of dresses," Pearl said politely. She was dying to see her own party frock. "Erm – did you have time to make one for me?"

Her grandmother clapped her floury

hands then wiped them on her apron. "Of course! How could I forget? Run upstairs, Red Riding-Hood. You will find the dress laid out on the bed."

"Thanks!" Pearl grinned then climbed the narrow stairs two at a time. She flung open the bedroom door. And . . .

"Oh!" she gasped. She looked around the room to make sure there was no mistake. No – there was only one party frock laid out on the bed, and it wasn't silver and sparkly.

"Try it on!" Red Riding-Hood's grandmother followed her up the stairs. "Let me see how it looks."

It looks . . . yucky! Pearl couldn't find the words to describe the shock frock. For a start, it was shiny and orange. *I'll look like a satsuma!* she groaned to herself.

Gran held up the dress and waited for Pearl to step into it.

The frock was way too big. It had a wide green sash and purple ribbons. The sleeves were like giant puffballs.

Her gran held up a mirror for her to see her reflection.

Orange and stiff, shiny and scratchy. Tight at the waist and droopy around the shoulders. *It's even worse than I thought!*

"Lovely!" Gran sighed. "Do a twirl, my dear."

Pearl twirled, hoping against hope that spinning round would whoosh her out of Red Riding-Hood world. *I can't go to the party looking like this!* she thought. *Everyone will laugh at me. Hans will make fun. Oh, help!*

Though she twirled until she was dizzy, her feet stayed firmly on the ground. There was no bright light to whisk her away.

"What do you think?" Gran asked, hands on hips and smiling from ear to ear.

Pearl took a deep breath. The orange

silk clashed with the colour of her hair. The green sash cut into her waist. The sleeves itched, the hem of the skirt went up and down like a roller-coaster. "It's . . ." she began.

". . . Perfect!" Gran decided. "You will be the belle of the ball. Now run along home, Red Riding-Hood, and help your mother get ready for the party!"

"Ouch!" Hans took one look at Pearl and shielded his eyes as if from a blinding light. "What happened? Did the sun fall from the sky? Is it a meteor dropping to earth?"

"Ha ha!" Pearl retorted.

"My grandmother made this dress for me, if you must know!"

Hans laughed until his stomach ached.

"Mum, do I have to wear this dress?" Pearl asked as she dashed into the cottage.

Tommy was dressed in his best baby bib and tucker. His cheeks shone.

"What dress?" Pearl's mum glanced over her shoulder. "Oh my!"

Pearl frowned. "That's what I mean – do I *have* to wear it?"

"Your grandmother would be upset if you didn't." Pearl's mum kept her face straight as she studied the effect. "It's very . . . unusual!"

"Everyone will laugh."

"But it's only for one day."

"One day too many." Pearl longed to get

out of the dress. "Please, Mum!"

"Keep it on and stop making a fuss." Briskly Pearl's mother picked up the baby and carried him outside. "Come and practise the maypole dance with Lydia and the other girls. Red Riding-Hood, do as I say!"

5

Oompah-oompah! Trumpets blared and drums banged as the girls rehearsed their dance on the village green.

Pearl held tight to a red ribbon attached to the top of the maypole and tried to follow instructions.

"Weave to your left, turn around and weave to your right!" Lydia told the girls as they danced. "No, Red Riding-Hood – I

said, weave to your *left*!"

"Ho-ho!" Hans sat on a stool and laughed himself silly.

Oompah! The band bellowed.

"Is everything ready?" Ploughman John ran across the green, chasing away stray ducks who had wandered up from the pond. "The Duke and Duchess are due to arrive very soon!"

"Where's your grandmamma?" Pearl's mother called.

"Here she comes!" Relieved to stop prancing around the maypole in her orange frock, Pearl scuttled off to meet Miller Brown's cart.

"Ah there you are, Red Riding-Hood!" Gran rode on the cart like a queen, the feathers in her red hat fluttering in the breeze.

"What a splendid sight!" Farmer Meade said, with a gleam in his eye and an extra bang on his big bass drum.

Pearl's grandmamma climbed down from the cart and saw that the village green was already full to bursting.

"Is there enough food?" Pearl's mother whispered to Lydia, who passed on the question to Gretchen, who was too busy smartening up the band to answer.

Oo-oompah! One of the trombones squeaked in surprise.

"Mum, there's enough food here to feed an army!" Pearl assured her. The tables groaned with the weight of goodies. "Hey, hands off!" she warned Hans as she caught him sneaking a cream bun.

"But where are the Duke and Duchess?" Pearl's grandma demanded. She stood at the very front of the crowd, waiting to curtsey.

"Coming now!" Ploughman John called from the edge of the green.

A gleaming purple carriage approached along the road that led down from the castle. It was pulled by four white horses in gold harnesses, wearing purple plumes of feathers on their proud heads.

The whole village held their breaths. Pearl caught a glimpse of the people

48

inside the carriage. The purple Duchess sat with her head held high, carrying a baby wrapped in a white lace christening gown. Beside her sat the bored Duke, twiddling the ends of his curled moustache.

The carriage stopped. A footman ran to open the door and the Duke and Duchess stepped out.

"Greetings, Your Graces!" Gran spoke for everyone. "We are honoured to welcome you."

The Duchess looked down her nose. Baby Max opened one eye. The Duke headed straight for the food.

"Take Max!" the Duchess said. Spying Pearl in her orange dress, she handed over the baby. "And mind you don't make him cry," she added as she went to join the Duke.

Pearl grimaced and kept tight hold of Max. His round face looked squashed and rubbery – not rosy and shiny like Tommy's.

"Strike up the band. Let the party begin!" Gran cried.

Oompah-pah-pah!

Baby Max looked startled.

"Dance, girls, dance!" Pearl's grandmother called.

Lydia led the village girls around the maypole.

Oo-oompah! Bish-bang-bang!

Max opened his mouth wide.

"Uh-oh!" Pearl rocked him back and forth. "Hush, don't cry!"

"Waa-aagh!" Max yelled above the trumpets and trombones.

"Hush!" Pearl pleaded. She held Max at arm's length.

Then the Duchess rushed over and snatched her baby. "There, there, my

darling!" she screeched. "Did the horrid girl make you cry?"

"Stop the music!" the Duke ordered.

The trombones whimpered and died.

"Waaaaagh!" Max went on yelling as if his lungs would burst.

"Cancel the party!" the Duke snapped as the Duchess carried Max back to the carriage. "From now until sunset, if anyone makes a sound, they shall be thrown in the dungeon!"

"B-b-but . . . !" Pearl's grandmother stammered. She was like a mighty ship with the wind taken out of its sails. "What shall we do with all this food?"

"Send it up to the castle, every last scrap!" the greedy Duke yelled as he slammed the door to the carriage behind him.

6

"I don't know why everyone blames me," Pearl said to Hans as they walked through the wood. She'd taken off her shock frock and changed into her striped skirt and clogs. "The second the band started to play, Max bawled. He doesn't like trumpets and stuff – I could've told you that if anyone had bothered to ask."

"I know – it's just that we were all

cheesed off," Hans explained. "We were looking forward to the party, so we blamed the nearest person and it just happened to be you, Red Riding-Hood."

"And I felt bad, believe me." Pearl hadn't expected Hans to be nice to her. But he'd been the first one to point out that it was the Duke and Duchess's fault that the party had been cancelled, not Pearl's. And he'd waited outside the cottage while she'd gone in and got changed before they took this walk across the meadow into the wood.

"We all know what the Duchess is like," Hans reminded her now. "High and mighty, hoity-toity, with never a good word to say about anyone."

"Hush!" The squirrels looked down from

their branches. "You never know who might be listening!"

"And the Duke!" Hans went on boldly. "He spends all his time hunting the poor deer instead of looking after his estate."

"Hush!" the rabbits warned, scurrying

for their burrows. "There are eyes and ears everywhere."

"Isn't it dangerous to say those things?" Pearl asked. "If the Duke and Duchess found out, they'd punish you."

Hans shrugged. He was still angry about the party. "So what? Every word is true, and I don't care who hears me."

"Foolish boy!" the birds in the trees whispered as Pearl and Hans walked on.

"I never was so disappointed!" Pearl's grandmother climbed the stile and entered the wood alone. She grumbled to herself as she made her way home. "Everyone dressed up in their finery, and the food prepared – tut-tut!"

Cunning eyes watched her toil along the

narrow path, her wide skirt brushing the bushes.

"All for nothing!" Gran went on. "And on such a lovely day, tut-tut!"

Silent paws padded after her, keeping to the shadows, waiting and watching.

"Do you really hate the Duke and Duchess?" Pearl asked Hans as they left the path and found a quiet clearing to sit in.

He nodded. "It's not fair. They're rich, yet they don't help the poor. They make their servants' lives unhappy, and they are miserable themselves."

"That's true," Pearl agreed. She'd never once seen the purple Duchess smile. Now she came to a big decision. "Listen, Hans – if I let you into a secret, do you promise to keep it?"

"I'm hot and bothered!" Pearl's grandmother sighed, fanning herself with a fern as she walked. "The sooner I reach home, the better!"

Not so fast! Crouching low, the yellow-eyed Wolf prepared to pounce on Gran.

His pink tongue lolled, his white teeth glistened.

All morning he'd lurked in the wood, watching preparations for the party from afar. His mouth had watered at the sight of meat pies. He'd licked his lips as the guests had arrived.

"Hot and bothered and let down," Gran complained, spying a fallen trunk where she could sit and rest. "Today is like Christmas that never comes!"

Wolfie crept closer – a grey shape with gleaming yellow eyes.

"What kind of secret?" Hans asked.

"It's about the Duke and his huntsmen," Pearl said. "They shot a stag and wounded him. If I show you, will you promise not to tell?"

"I swear!" Hans replied.

At last Wolfie pounced.

Pearl's gran saw his white teeth and snarling lips. "Help!" she cried.

"What was that?" Hans heard the scream as Pearl led him towards the overhanging rock where the wounded stag was hidden.

"Help!" came a second cry.

"It's Gran!" Pearl gasped, forgetting the stag and racing towards the sound.

They heard the Wolf's roar and caught glimpses of Gran's bright red bodice and blue skirt between the trees. Hearts pounding, Pearl and Hans raced towards the spot.

7

Gran fought back.

As Wolfie pounced, she kicked and yelled. She gripped him by the scruff of the neck and shook him until his teeth rattled.

"Hang on, Gran, we'll save you!" Pearl yelled. Her grandmother was wrestling with the Wolf, rolling over and over in the undergrowth.

Whack! Gran gave Wolfie a great big

smack around the chops.

"Wrraaagh!" he roared. He wriggled out of the old woman's grasp and tried to catch his breath.

"Steady!" Hans warned Pearl as they drew near. "Watch out Wolfie doesn't turn on us!"

Pearl nodded, her eyes on her gran. "Don't move, Grandmamma."

The Wolf panted and crouched low, ears pricked and ready to attack again. He'd almost had the plump old woman in his grasp – but not quite.

Now two nosey children were set to interfere with his supper. He whined at them and bared his fangs.

"And wait for him to pounce again? Not likely!" Grandma ignored Pearl's advice.

She raised the basket that she'd been carrying and began to bash Wolfie around the head.

Whack-smack-bash! Wolfie was too slow. He felt the blows rain down.

"Careful!" Pearl cried. This wasn't the way it was supposed to happen in the what-big-eyes-ears-and-teeth-you-have part of the story.

"Watch out – he's trying to grab your leg!" Hans warned.

"Oh no you don't!" Gran kept up the attack until Wolfie cowered against a tree trunk. "Take that!" she cried. "And that. And that!"

"And that was the end of it!" Pearl's grandmother told Farmer Meade, dusting herself down.

The stout old man had come huffing and puffing across the meadow as soon as he'd heard screams from the wood. He arrived just as Gran had trapped Wolfie against the tree and given him one final whack to send him packing.

"Absolutely magnificent!" Farmer

Meade murmured after he'd listened to her account.

"Yes. Gran didn't need saving after all." Pearl felt a little disappointed. "She can stick up for herself, no problem."

"You should have seen the look on Wolfie's face!" Hans laughed. "By the time we got here, he'd gone cross-eyed!"

"Your grandmother is a remarkable woman," the farmer told Pearl.

"But the Wolf got away to fight another day, more's the pity." Pearl's gran brushed leaves and grass from her skirt and straightened her petticoats.

Farmer Meade offered to take her arm. "Please let me escort you to your cottage door."

"That's OK. Hans and I can do

that!" Pearl said quickly.

But Pearl's gran tilted her head and smiled coyly. "Why, Farmer Meade, that is very kind." She took his arm graciously.

"B-but!" Pearl was caught off-guard and didn't get it – why was Farmer Meade so keen to step in?

She felt Hans grab her hand and tug her away. "Come on, slow-coach!"

And, yank, she was whisked away through the wood, still tutting, as the old farmer and her gran walked on together.

"So what about the secret?" Hans asked, laughing as usual. "You know – the one you were about to show me?"

"Oh, that!" It came flooding back – the cruel hunters and the wounded stag in his den. The faithful doe standing guard. "I've still got time to take you there. Come on, let's go!"

But they had only gone a few steps before there was a rustling in the bushes and a family of rabbits raced across their path.

"Run!" they cried. "Make haste! The Wolf is near!"

Pearl and Hans watched the frightened rabbits disappear into some long grass. They saw a pheasant flap her wings and rise noisily from among the ferns. Then two squirrels fled up a nearby trunk.

Pearl frowned and hurried forward until they drew close to the stag's hiding place.

"What's wrong?" Hans asked when she stopped and looked around.

"I'm wondering what happened to the

doe," she whispered. "She should be keeping a lookout."

But the wood was silent and shadowy, empty of all the creatures who lived close by.

Suddenly there was a crashing sound and the missing doe bounded out of the willow bushes. Her eyes were wild with fear. "Too late!" she cried.

Pearl's heart thudded. "What do you mean? What happened?" Without thinking, she ran forward to the overhanging rock and thrust aside the branches that hid the stag from view. Her spirits plunged as she saw that the den was empty.

"He's gone!" the doe sighed.

"Where to?" Pearl ran here and there,

searching for her wounded friend. "Tell me what happened!"

The doe's eyes filled with tears. "The Wolf found us. First I heard a fight on the far side of the wood. There were human cries and the roar of an angry wolf."

"We know about that," Hans cut in.

"Afterwards, I listened. There was a silence in the wood which I did not like."

"Did the stag know that Wolfie was nearby?" Pearl asked.

The doe shook her head. "I peered between the willow branches and saw that he was sleeping to gather his strength. I did not disturb him because I believed he was safely hidden. Instead, I crossed the stream to search on the far bank. When I returned, the den was empty."

"And you panicked?" Pearl asked. She turned to Hans. "The poor stag was badly hurt. He was resting here until he was stronger."

"What do you think happened to him?" Hans asked the unhappy doe. "Do you suppose the Wolf found him after all?"

She nodded. "He was weak. He could not run fast."

"But there's no sign of a fight," Pearl pointed out, her hopes rising until she found a tuft of grey fur attached to the spike of a thorn bush. Then she spotted paw prints like those of a large dog in the soft mud. "Wolfie was definitely here," she muttered.

"Look at these deer tracks!" Hans had discovered a set of prints that led up the slope.

"Are you thinking what I'm thinking? That Wolfie tracked down the stag, but the stag managed to escape?"

Hans nodded. "The question is, how far could he manage to run before Wolfie caught up with him?"

"Not far," the doe sighed.

But Pearl refused to listen. "We don't know that for sure. We have to follow the tracks and find out."

"I'm with you," Hans agreed, inviting Pearl to scramble up the rock to join him.

He waited for her to catch her breath. "Ready?"

"Let's go!" she said to Hans and the doe. "And we won't stop until we find him!"

8

"Yes, that is the way!" The squirrels chattered excitedly. "Follow the tracks!"

"Make haste!" the rabbits cried.

Pearl and Hans stumbled through the thick undergrowth as the doe ran on ahead. They struggled up the hill towards the Duke and Duchess's castle.

"The stag is growing weaker," a fox reported. "My cousin the Wolf is hard on his heels."

The stag's tracks had vanished in the middle of some long grass, so Pearl stopped to talk to the fox. "Which way now?" she demanded.

The fox fixed her with a cold stare. His eyes were yellow and sly like Wolfie's.

"Come on, tell us!" Pearl pleaded. She knew time was running out for her brave friend.

"I will not help you," the fox replied. "Let the foolish rabbits and squirrels, the slippery frogs and slow hedgehogs show you the way!" And he flicked the white tip of his bushy tail before darting off down the hill.

Meanwhile Hans ran towards a stream and found new tracks on the muddy bank.

"Over here!" he called. He showed Pearl the deep prints in the mud. "Here are the tracks of the stag, and over here are the Wolf's paw prints."

"Maybe the stag stopped to drink and this is where Wolfie finally caught up with him," Pearl said then stopped short. She was out of breath and too scared to picture what might have happened next.

"You're right," a frog croaked from a nearby rock. "I saw it. The stag seemed too weak to go on. He needed to rest. But when the Wolf pounced he fought back and drove him off with his mighty antlers."

"Thank goodness!" Pearl sighed. She gathered her own strength, thanking the frog and asking which way the stag had gone.

"Up the hill into the forest," the frog told her, glistening green and gold in the sunlight. "And look, here comes the doe to show you the way!"

Sure enough, the doe bounded back down the hill. "Come quickly!" she cried.

So Pearl and Hans followed the frightened doe, their hearts beating fast, into the forest and to the shadows of the high castle walls, where they found the stag and the Wolf at last.

The stag's head was down. He thrust at Wolfie with his antlers. The cunning Wolf had backed him against the stone wall. It seemed there was no escape.

Wolfie snarled. His ears were back, the hair at the scruff of his neck stood proud. He didn't see Pearl and Hans approach from behind.

The stag lunged at Wolfie with his mighty antlers, but he was weak and the Wolf easily dodged aside. The stag stumbled and fell to his knees.

Then Wolfie spun round. His jaws snapped at the stag's legs, missing by a hair's breadth.

"No you don't!" Pearl and Hans yelled, arming themselves with heavy sticks

and falling on Wolfie.

"If Gran can do this, so can we!" Pearl cried.

So they bashed and beat the Wolf as he bared his teeth and snapped, furious to be cheated of his supper yet again.

The doe joined the stag, nosing and nudging him back on to his feet. "Try to run," she murmured.

With his final shred of courage and strength, the great creature rose.

The Wolf howled under Hans and Pearl's blows.

The stag raised his mighty head.

"Flee!" the doe urged again.

Wolfie rolled and writhed in the shadow of the castle wall. The stag gazed around – at the tumbling stream, the tall trees and safety, at the children struggling with the Wolf under the looming castle walls. His weak legs trembled, his sides heaved, but there was a determined look in his dark eyes as he turned towards the stream.

"Go!" Pearl cried as she whacked Wolfie with a branch.

And with one great leap, the stag soared over the glittering stream, landed on the far bank and fled deep into the forest.

"Take that and it serves you right!" Pearl kept Wolfie trapped against the castle wall while the stag escaped.

The Wolf had twigs tangled in his fur and thorns deep in his paws. He whined and yelped.

"Have you had enough?" Pearl demanded. "Do you promise not to chase the stag ever again?"

"I promise," the sly, cheating Wolf whined as he slunk away.

Just then, there was a clamour at the entrance to the castle. The gates flew open and a band of men rode out.

"It's the Duke and his hunters!" Hans cried, recognising the Duke's long moustache under the brim of his feathered hunting hat. "They must have spotted the stag from the top of the castle wall!"

The hunters blew their horns. Birds rose from the trees and flew away.

"Aha!" the Duke cried, spying Hans and Pearl. "Which way did the stag go, tell me quick!"

Before Hans could stop her, Pearl ran up to the Duke and stood in his horse's path. "Turn back!" she told him. "If you must chase something, tell your men to hunt the Wolf and save the villagers!"

The Duke's white horse reared up. Its golden bridle jingled. "Stand aside!" the Duke hissed.

"Never!" Pearl vowed.

From a distance, Hans ducked behind a bush and blocked his ears. "I don't want to hear this!" he muttered.

"I'll never stand aside and let you hunt down the beautiful stag!" Pearl cried, laying hold of the Duke's reins.

The hunters let their horns fall to their sides. They sat open-mouthed as Pearl defied the Duke.

"He's my friend. I don't care what you do to me – I won't let go of these reins!"

"Who is this wretched girl?" the Duke demanded.

"She is no one," a hunter told him. "Just a child from the village."

"And is she mad to stand in my way?" The Duke tried to pull free but Pearl hung on.

Hans peered through the bush. "Mad as a March hare!" he groaned.

"I won't let go!" Pearl insisted as two

huntsmen dismounted and ran to take hold of her.

"Seize her!" the Duke yelled. "This little nobody has delayed us and spoiled a good hunt."

"Yes, Your Grace." The men grappled with Pearl as the Duke broke free and turned his horse back towards the courtyard. "There is no point in struggling," they warned her.

The Duke disappeared through the castle gates without even looking over his shoulder. "Throw her in the dungeon and give her nothing to eat or drink!" he cried.

"Mad as a hatter!" Hans muttered from his hiding place. "Red Riding-Hood is out of her tiny mind!"

9

The huntsmen rushed Pearl across the courtyard and down stone steps into a dark corridor. From way above, in one of the grand gold and purple rooms of the castle, came the sound of Baby Max bawling.

"Why are you back so soon?" Pearl heard the Duchess ask the Duke.

"A foolish girl stood in our way and the

hunt was ruined," the Duke snapped back. "Now what's for dinner? I'm hungry!"

Pearl was hauled down the corridor to a heavy wooden door. One of the men turned a rusty key and it creaked open. *Yuck!* It seemed Pearl would be spending her time with spiders and rats.

"Let me light a candle," the second man said, going in ahead of Pearl. "I feel sorry for the child, having to end her days in this dark place."

Pearl shuddered. The cell was cold and damp, with only a low wooden bed and a straw mattress.

"Come away," the first man told his companion harshly. "And remind me to tell the jailer – no food or drink!"

Slam! The door closed and Pearl heard

the key turn in the lock. *At least I saved the stag's life*, she thought, drawing her cloak around her. *Three times, actually.* She was pleased she'd been brave enough to do that. *But look where I ended up!*

Wearily Pearl gazed at the rough stone walls and arched roof. She poked the mattress and found that it was hard. A rat scuttled out from under the bed.

"Oh!" Pearl cried.

The rat sat in the middle of the dirty floor. He licked his paws and cleaned his whiskers. "No need to sound so surprised," he scolded. "I'm the one who has to put up with an unwelcome guest, I'll have you know."

"S-sorry," Pearl stammered. "Of course, this is your room."

"Exactly!" the rat agreed, twitching his long pink tail. "I've lived here in this dungeon all my life, and they never bother to ask me whether I'd like to share the place, oh no! That would be too much to expect."

Pearl swallowed hard. "So what happened to the last person who was here?"

The rat tutted. "I don't know and I don't care. The fellow spent six weeks here with me and never spoke a civil word. Grunts and groans were all I got."

Pearl frowned then sat on the edge of the bed. "I expect he was unhappy."

"What's happiness got to do with anything?" the rat demanded. "Do you think I'm happy to spend my time scuttling around in search of the Duke's leftover scraps? Am I happy getting chased out of the kitchen by the Duchess's fat black cat?"

"No, I suppose not." Studying the rat more closely, Pearl saw that he was quite thin.

"And are the mighty Duke and Duchess happy, even though they have everything?" the rat continued. "I don't think so! Oh no – you just have to look at the Duchess's haughty, pinched face to see that she's one of the unhappiest women alive. As for the Duke, he eats every scrap on his plate and leaves nothing for anyone else."

"I stopped the Duke from hunting the stag," Pearl confessed. "That's why he put me here."

The rat looked at Pearl with more

respect. "Good for you."

"But this is where it landed me," Pearl sighed. "I'm stuck here and now I have no way of getting back home – my *real* home – even if I wanted to."

"And where's your real home?" the rat asked, jumping on to the bed beside her.

"It's a long way away – you wouldn't understand." She thought of Amber and Lily waiting for her beside the magic dressing-up box, of the questions her worried mum would ask when she came to collect her. *It's my own fault – I was the one who couldn't wait to get back to Red Riding-Hood world*, she sighed to herself.

"Try me," the rat invited, settling on the mattress. "Come along, tell me your story – we have all the time in the world!"

10

"Red Riding-Hood is a good girl," Gran told Hans as she climbed the steps up to the castle next day. "But sometimes she acts hastily and doesn't stop to think."

"You don't have to tell me," Hans sighed.

The day before he'd watched the huntsmen drag Pearl off to the dungeons then raced down the hill to the village.

He'd sought out Pearl's grandmamma and told her everything.

"Now the Duke will let her starve!" he'd cried. "You have to help me get her out of there!"

Pearl's gran had sat down and thought hard. "Go home," she'd told Hans. "Tell Red Riding-Hood's mother that she is staying with me for the night, so as not to alarm her. Tomorrow at dawn I will meet you at the foot of the castle steps."

So here they were, approaching the castle as the sun rose, carrying two large, carefully wrapped parcels.

"What's in the packages?" Hans asked Gran.

"Wait and see," she said, huffing and puffing up the steps.

"And what's your plan?" he asked. But he knew he wouldn't be told.

"As I said, you must wait and see," Gran puffed, tapping the side of her nose.

Rat-a-tat-tat! Boldly Hans knocked at the castle gate.

"I didn't sleep a wink!" Pearl groaned.

"Nonsense, you kept me awake all night with your snoring," Ratty told her. He'd already been out looking for breakfast. "Here, have a nibble at this," he invited.

Cautiously Pearl took the small piece of dry bread from his paws. She held it up to the candle and inspected it.

"Eat up. Beggars can't be choosers."

"You're right," she said, and gulped down the food gratefully. "And thank you

very much." she added.

"Not at all," the rat said, munching at a scrap of the Duke's bacon rind. "Guess what I heard from the sparrows in the gutter?"

"What?"

"Your grandmother and a boy named Hans are knocking at the castle door."

Pearl's heart leaped. "Are you sure?"

"It's what the sparrows said and they

should know," the rat shot back. "There's nothing like a bird's eye view of the world."

"Yes?" A footman opened the door and peered out.

"We've come to talk to the Duke," Gran announced.

"He won't see you," the footman replied.

"Tell him that we bring gifts."

The door opened a fraction wider. "What kind of gifts?"

"Gifts made by my own fair hand!" Gran said grandly. "Delicious, gorgeous gifts.Tell him!"

So the servant went off with the message while Hans shifted uneasily from one foot to the other. *These gifts had better be good if they're going to get Red Riding-Hood out of jail,* he thought.

"Enter!" the footman said when he came back. "The Duke will see you in the breakfast room."

Up the stairs along a grand corridor, bearing gifts for the Duke and Duchess, Gran marched on.

"Good morning, Your Grace! How are you on this beautiful sunny day?"

"Humph!" he grunted, his back to them.

"Now I know Your Grace has a sweet tooth," Gran went on as she unwrapped

94

the first parcel. A beautiful smell of fresh baking began to emerge. "And no one makes a fruit cake as well as me. I bake it with butter from my daughter's best cow and with the finest flour. The eggs are laid fresh every day by my white hen."

Slowly the Duke turned to face her. "Hmm . . ." he sniffed and his nose led him forward.

"In this cake there are raisins and cherries, orange peel and cinnamon. And sugar, Your Grace. *Lots* of sugar!"

"What's the catch?" the Duke asked as he stood with his knife poised over the cake.

"No catch," Gran insisted. "I will bring Your Grace

such a cake every day of the week, just as long as you do me one small favour."

The knife quivered in the Duke's hand. "Name it!"

"That you will release my poor Little Red Riding-Hood from your dungeon," Gran said, smiling sweetly, one hand on the cake, ready to whisk it from under the Duke's nose. "After all, she is only a young, foolish girl who knows no better!"

"Madam, you are trying to bribe me!" the Duke retorted, aware that the Duchess had crept quietly into the room. Without this interruption he would have given way instantly.

"Egbert, what do these people want?" his wife asked.

Uh-oh, that's the end of that! Hans groaned.

But Gran turned round and curtseyed low. "Give me the other parcel!" she whispered to Hans. "I have brought Your Grace a gift!" she cooed. The paper rustled as she unpacked the present.

"What is it?" the Duchess moved in close.

"A gown made of the finest purple silk, Your Grace. I sewed it with my own fair hands. The neck is low-cut to show off your white skin, the waist is tiny, the skirt full!"

What a fright! Hans cringed. Frills and flounces, ribbons and bows. *This'll never work.*

"Hmm." The Duchess's fingertips

touched the shiny silk. She almost smiled as she held the gown up against her. "How do I look?"

"Perfect!" Gran cooed again. "Nobody in the whole world can match your beauty in that gown, Your Grace!"

Down in the dungeon, Pearl kept her fingers crossed.

"I see that no sooner do you get here than you are anxious to leave," Ratty complained, sniffing and stroking his whiskers. "What is it that you don't like about my humble room?"

"The fact that the door is locked," Pearl

pointed out. "This is a prison, you know."

"For some." Ratty sighed and stroked his whiskers. "But for me it is the place I call home!"

"Well?" the Duke asked his wife. "Shall you keep the dress?"

"On condition that you set Red Riding-Hood free," Gran reminded her. "If you give me my grandchild back, I will sew you as many gowns as you please."

"Hmm," the Duchess said, holding up the dress and giving a thoughtful twirl.

Hans glanced at Gran and crossed his fingers. From the nursery next door Max bawled and wailed.

"Bless me, that child has a fine pair of lungs!" Gran cried, suddenly dashing off.

She came back juggling the baby on her hip. "Cootchy-coo! Google-google-goo!"

Max looked surprised. His little hands clutched at Gran's lace collar as she rocked him then swung him round. *Waagh-waagh-whoo-weee!*

"Who's my favourite boy?" Gran cootchy-cooed. "Little Max, that's who!"

Waagh-weeeee! Max stopped crying.

"'Diddle-diddle dumpling, my son John!'" Gran sang.

Giggle-giggle!

"'Went to bed with his trousers on.

One shoe off and one shoe on,

Diddle-diddle dumpling, my son John!'"

"Look, Griselda, Max is smiling!" the Duke cried.

Ah now, that's more like it! Hans grinned

100

to himself. *Forget the cake and the fancy frock – this hits the spot!*

Gran cuddled Max close and kissed his cheeks. "Who's a good, *good* little boy!"

"S-s-smiling?" The Duchess crept close to Gran. "Yes, you are right! Old woman, you must come every day and make Max smile. You must be his nursemaid!"

"I must, must I?" Gran said slowly. With her back to the Duke and Duchess, she winked at Hans.

"Every day!" the Duchess insisted, realising in an instant what she had to do to get the clever old woman to agree. "Egbert, release Red Riding-Hood from the dungeon immediately! Send her home to her mother this very second!"

11

"I'm glad everything's back to normal," Pearl told the stag.

They'd let her out of the dungeon, thanks to Gran and Hans, and she'd gone home to her mum and Tommy as if nothing had happened. Now every day Gran went up to the castle in her best clothes. She looked after Max and bossed everyone to her heart's content.

"Mind you, Hans is never going to let me forget what an idiot I was!"

The stag shook his head. "You saved my life. You allowed me to escape from the Wolf and the Duke. I will always remember that."

Pearl smiled then sighed. She looked out across the hillsides at the setting sun. "Are you better?" she asked.

"As strong as ever, thanks to you." The stag stood proudly in the shadows. There was a long silence then he said, "Why are you sad?"

"Because . . ." How could she explain that she was homesick?

"Because all is not what it seems and you long to return to your real home?" he asked in his deep, calm voice.

Pearl blinked. "How did you know?"

"The rat explained to the sparrows, who flew into the forest and told the doe. The doe told me your whole story."

"I see." She leaned against a tree. "It looks like I'm stuck here for good this time."

The stag looked down kindly at her. "Where are you going now, Red Riding-Hood?"

"To meet Grandmamma at the castle gate. I'm taking her some of the special butter that she likes, and my mother's ginger biscuits."

"Why don't you sit for a while?" the stag suggested. "Take out a biscuit. Taste it. Is it good?"

Pearl munched on the gingerbread pig.

"Very good!"

"Close your eyes."

"Mmmm . . . delicious!"

"Watch out, here she comes!" Lily yelled.

Amber's basement filled with dazzling light. The smell of home baking wafted through the window on a warm breeze.

"We hope!" Amber gasped. Pearl had been gone for what seemed like ages. Amber and Lily had begun to think she would never come back.

The light filled the room. There was a whoosh.

"Home at last!" Pearl cried.

*

"The stag told me to bite the gingerbread pig and whoosh!" Pearl told Lily and Amber. "I got the dizzy thing and the bright light, then I started to float."

"And here you are!" Amber grinned. "Wolfie didn't get you after all."

"Almost but not quite." Pearl had lots to tell them as she took off her striped skirt and red clogs. "I was worried he'd get Gran and then the stag. You can't trust a single thing he says . . ."

"Whoa!" Lily stopped her. "What do you mean – do the stag and Wolfie talk?"

"Of course. And the rabbits and the squirrels – everyone!"

"Wow, talking animals!" Amber was jealous. "What else?"

"The Duke and Duchess threw a party. There was maypole dancing and a brass band. Loads of food."

"And what did you wear?" Lily asked. "Did you have a new dress?"

Carefully Pearl stashed her Red Riding-Hood clothes into a corner of the dressing-up box. "Ah, the party frock," she sighed. "It wasn't exactly what I'd hoped for, but I definitely made a big impression – that's for sure!"

Have you checked out...

www.dressingupdreams.net

It's the place to go for games, downloads, activities, sneak previews and lots of fun!

You'll find a special dressing-up game and lots of activities and fun things to do, as well as news on Dressing-Up Dreams and all your favourite characters.

Sign up to the newsletter at **www.dressingupdreams.net** to receive extra clothes for your Dressing-Up Dreams doll and the opportunity to enter special members only competitions.

What happens next...?

Log onto www.dressingupdreams.net for a sneak preview of my next adventure!

WIN A *Dressing-Up Dreams* GOODIE BAG!

CAN YOU SPOT THE TWO DIFFERENCES AND THE HIDDEN LETTER IN THESE TWO PICTURES OF PEARL?

There is a spot-the-difference picture and hidden letter in the back of all four Dressing-Up Dreams books about Pearl (look for the books with 9 to 12 on the spine). Hidden in one of the pictures above is a secret letter. Find all four letters and put them together to make a special Dressing-Up Dreams word, then send it to us. Each month, we will put the correct entries in a draw and one lucky winner will receive a magical Dressing-Up Dreams goodie bag including an exclusive Dressing-Up Dreams keyring!

Send your magical word, your name, age and your address on a postcard to: **Pearl's Dressing-Up Dreams Competition**

UK Readers:
Hodder Children's Books
338 Euston Road
London NW1 3BH
kidsmarketing@hodder.co.uk

Australian Readers:
Hachette Children's Books
Level 17/207 Kent Street
Sydney NSW 2000
childrens.books@hachette.com.au

New Zealand Readers:
Hachette Livre NZ Ltd
PO Box 100 749
North Shore City 0745
childrensbooks@hachette.co.nz

Only one entry per child. Final draw: 30th March 2010
For full terms and conditions go to http://www.hodderchildrens.co.uk/Terms_and_Conditions.htm

COLOURING FUN!

Carefully colour the Dressing-Up Dreams picture on the next page and then send it in to us.

Or you can draw your very own fairytale character. You might want to think about what they would wear or if they have special powers.

Each month, we will put the best entries on the website gallery and one lucky winner will receive a magical Dressing-Up Dreams goodie bag!

Send your drawing,
your name, age and address on a postcard to:
Pearl's Dressing-Up Dreams Competition

UK Readers:	**Australian Readers:**	**New Zealand Readers:**
Hodder Children's Books	Hachette Children's Books	Hachette Livre NZ Ltd
338 Euston Road	Level 17/207 Kent Street	PO Box 100 749
London NW1 3BH	Sydney NSW 2000	North Shore City 0745
kidsmarketing@hodder.co.uk	childrens.books@hachette.com.au	childrensbooks@hachette.co.nz

Pearl's party frock

The Woodcutter's Son

cut along the lines marked with ✂

SLOT CHARACTER INTO STAND